When the Wind Blows...

Cecilia "CJ" Johnson and Sasha D Robinson

Published by Sasha Robinson, 2024.

WHEN THE WIND BLOWS...

First edition. March 29, 2024.

Copyright © 2024 Cecilia "CJ" Johnson and Sasha D Robinson.

ISBN: 979-8224697519

Written by Cecilia "CJ" Johnson and Sasha D Robinson.

Table of Contents

I dedicate this to Jibri Omari Jones,

When the wind blows......
by Sasha D. Robinson
Quez's voice

"Whenever you feel a soft gentle breeze, it is a loved one who passed away letting you know it is ok, or so I have heard. Since I have been a kid, I used to wonder are there such things as ghosts? Are they partying with celebrities? Is there an afterlife where people who die, do they actually watch us? If they are, then when it is my time to go, I know many of my friends and families who died have seen my whole life and I am not looking forward to that meeting."

Marquez or Quez, a mid 40's year-old African-American man wearing a graphic tee-shirt and kahki shorts, gets out of his blue four door sedan on a beautiful day in Texas.

As he put on his sunglasses, Quez walks across the green grass and the weather gets over 90 degrees but on this Saturday afternoon, it is in the mid 80's and it feels great to be outside. As he walked through the greenest grass, he observes people talking to each other but it is as quiet as a christmas night.

"Hey old friend," Quez said as he stared at a headstore.

The headstone reads *"Here lies Carter Miles Johnson: A son and friend."*

"It's been a couple of months and you would not believe what all that has been going on in my life," Quez said as he bent down to wipe the dirt from the headstone to where you are able to March 10, 1978 - December 11, 2000. "I met this woman a couple of weeks ago and for the first time, I think she is the one."

Quez glances up from the headstone and started watching other people at the cemetary talking to missed loved ones and then remove his shades. As a warm gentle breeze blew around him, there was nothing but silence in the cemetary despite many people are around and birds are seen flying around,

"I honestly think the good Lord brought her to me because her birthday is the same as yours and she loves Star Wars," he said as he started to wipe the tears from his eyes. "Cause if you did, thank you. The other day, I took her to a Spurs game and for some reason I thought about the time we went to get playoff tickets. Man we were stupid."

Quez let out a chuckle closed his eyes and looked up at the the clouds in the blue sky and let out a sigh.

"I am surprised we were able to go," Quez said.

"Hey Quez, I knew you were going to be here," said a voice from the distance.

Quez turned around and saw a middle aged black man with a full black and gray beard walking towards him wearing a white t-shirt and basketball shorts.

"Hey Marlon," Quez said. "I was not expecting to see you until tonight. Why are you here?"

As Marlon walked closer to Quez, they gave each other a "bro hug" and turn around to face Carter's headstone.

"You aren't the only one who can come and visit an old friend," Marlon said while he was trying to brandish a smile. "Plus I knew you were going to be here."

Quez's happiness to seeing Marlon changed to a quizzical look as he slowly turned around to face Carter's headstone.

"What do you mean you knew I was going to be here," Quez said.

"You always come and see Carter when you come into town, I was trying to meet up with you cause you weren't answering your phone," Marlon said as he reaches in his pocket to get a packet of tissue to wipe the tears from his face. "Tommy is on his way and we are going to get something to eat. Did you want to go with us?"

Quez's quizzical look disappears to a smile as he closes his eyes during another gentle warm breeze touches his face.

"Where are you guys going to eat?" Quez asked.

"We are going to Carter's to watch the NBA playoffs," Marlon said. "I think famous sports show host would bring the restaraunt some faces also."

Quez would start to laugh at Marlon.

"Negro I am not famous," Quez said. "I just interview some people and have a radio show."

"Fool, you've been on press row for the Super Bowl and got to interview people on NBA All-Star Weekend," Marlon said as he laughs. "You are famous."

The two men laugh for a moment and then silence fell upon the two.

"I miss him, Quez," Marlon said as he cries. "I miss him bro. What gets me the most is he was strong enough to live long even though he lived most of his life with cancer. He was good."

As Marlon continues to cry, Quez put his arm around him for a brief moment to console him.

"Thanks bro," Marlon said as he wipes the tears from his face again. "I think it is fate we will all be here today."

"Yeah," Quez said very low close to a whisper.

"Man we grew up together, had some adventures, got in trouble and hell was in Omari's wedding," Marlon said. "Hell, I remember the day we all met."

Quez starts to laugh and look at Marlon.

"I was about to talk to Carter about this," Quez said as he smiles, closes his eyes and look up to the sky and feel another gentle breeze.

April 27, 1994

Quez's voice:

The sun was barely coming through the clouds on this normal morning before school starts. This was your average high school that had the cliched cliques from the snobs, jocks, nerds, mean girls and gang members. Yet on this morning not a lot of students were here are here because school started at 8 a.m. but I got to school around 7:15 a.m. In my sophomore year, I was a 5'7 15 years old athletic build young black man who played football for the school and was encouraged not to do anything outside of athletics to prevent an injury but guess what, me and my friend Tommy was playing a pick up basketball game to impress some of the girls especially and my high school crush, Macy Daniels. Tommy who was just as athletic as anyone did not play sports because his filipino parents and background are adimant about him focusing more on his studies instead of doing extra curricular activites. After my team beat the other team, I looked up and saw Macy sitting down with a bunch of her friends and I was in awe. Her caramel colored skin, curly hair and smile had me from the first time I saw her. Too bad she had a boyfriend. Macy was dating the star point guard for the JV Basketball team, Marlon Braxton and I thought he was a jerk. Marlon sat up from sitting next to her while she was laughing with her friends.

"Who got next?" Tommy asked as Quez was catching his breath and get some water from a water bottle that was on the sideline next to his backpack.

As Marlon stood up, he took off his dress shirt.

"Yo, me and my boy are up," Marlon said as he started to take his t-shirt and put on his school gym shirt. Marlon looked opposite from where he was 20 years ago. When His athletic frame showed as he switched shirts and took his jeans off because he wore his gym shorts. "Lets make this four on four."

"Alright," Quez said after he takes a jump shot.

Marlon and a couple of guys walked to on the court and grabbed the rebound from Quez's missed shot and started to dribble around and do a behind the back pass to one of his teammates.

"This ain't football homeboy," Marlon said. "When you walk on this court, you come into my world and I will make you my bitch."

All of the teens on the court started to laugh while Quez stood there with an angry look on his face.

"Whatever negro," Quez said as he looked around to see if the rest of his team is on the court. "Winner takes it out and I am going to ruin you like Mitch Richmond did to the Spurs a couple of years ago."

The two teams start to play their game up to 15 and through out the game, Quez was making the game against Marlon personal. Marlon did a cross-over move on Quez and laid the ball up for a basket, and did a hand sign as Macy jumped up to cheer and did the same hand sign.

"9 to 7," Marlon said as he is trying to catch his breath, Marlon said. "I'm MJ and you're Craig Ehlo. Told you I am going to own you."

Quez walks up to Marlon and started to face guard him so he can prevent him from getting the ball as his teammate tried to inbound the ball to him. Quez would steal the ball and his team would set up their offense.

"Well Craig Ehlo is about to put you on Sports Center," Quez said before he made a spin move and then passed the ball to Tommy who was cutting to the basket for a quick lay up.

"9-8, now get ready for us to have you go back to the gym," Tommy said as everyone was starting to set up to take the ball out. While the game was going on, Carter, who is a 14-year old skinny African American male who walks with a slight lean is walking up to the basketball court but stopped by Omari, a tall and skinny 14-year old African American male.

"Are we really going to do it," Carter shockingly asked Omari.

"Yes," Omari said as he pulled out what looks to be a bus schedule. "The bus comes at 7:50 and if we get to the Alamodome by 8:30 get the tickets and then be back by third period."

"How are we going to get there?" Carter asks as the two teenagers start to walk towards the basketball court.

"I am going to ask my sister to take us," Omari said as they start to usher there way through a crowd of students. The two stop and watch the basketball game between Quez and Marlon's team.

"What the hell is Marlon doing out there," Carter asks while he started to watch the game as Omari glanced at his watch.

The game started to get more intense where Marlon's team had the ball. The game drew a bigger crowd than it was before but it was probably because both Marlon and Quez are both talking noise on the court. After making a move to get to the basket, Quez fouls Marlon that causes him to fall to the ground.

"Bitch, what the fuck is your damn problem?" Marlon said as he jumped back up and charged at Quez.

"That was on accident, but if you weren't faking in front of your broad maybe you would be a better player," Quez yelled back to Marlon.

Tommy seperated Quez and Marlon while his teammates dragged him to the sideline.

"Fuck you bitch," Marlon yelled back to Quez.

Macy ran over to Marlon and dragged him back to the sidelines while Tommy took Quez to get his things and the two walked towards the building.

"It is ok man," Tommy said while trying to catch his breath. "What the hell is wrong with you. Man if the coaches find out about this, you know you going to get it."

"Man fuck him and that bitch," Quez yelled in anger. "He is lucky everyone broke it up cause I would have fucked him up."

As Tommy and Quez walked in the school building, Carter and Omari are behind them trying to hurry up to make it to the other side of the school where the bus stop is at. Omari reached out to grab Quez's shoulder to stop him.

"What did Macy do to you," Omari ask Quez as the two stopped to talk to in the hallway of the school. "She is my friend and I never heard her do anything wrong to anyone"

"Man I don't have a problem with her," Quez told Omari as he was trying to calm down from being angry. "I just don't like her".

As Quez and Tommy starts to walk down the hallway while, the other two walked behind them.

"Why don't you like her?" Omari asked. "I mean I understand you getting humiliated by Marlon on the court but it doesn't make sense to call Macy a bitch."

Quez calm demeaner started to get angry again and looked at Omari. Even though he is a year younger than him, Omari stood 5'10 so when Quez went turned around to get in his face, he had glance up to look into his eyes.

"I don't have a problem with that bitch," Quez yelled. "Why you trying to save that hoe. Damn, why don't you take your cape off and quit trying to save these hoes."

Omari laughed at Quez.

"Did you just try to quote E-40?," Omari said as his laughter was coming down. "Man stop it. I am not in the mood. I am just want to know why you calling her a bitch and hoes but she didn't do anything"

Quez looks at Omari square in the eye as he noticed Omari's tall, lanky frame was not backing down from the more athletic and muscular built teen. Quez would relax his aggressive posture as Carter and Tommy were on each of their sides to make sure they did not fight. Omari would put his hands on Carter's shoulder to let him know everything is alright.

"Hey C, it is ok," Omari said as he stared at Quez. "I have an older sister that whooped me up and down the street, I am not going to let you intimidate me."

Everyone stops for a moment to look at each other and then looks at Omari.

"What the hell did you say?" Tommy asked. "Your sister busted your ass?"

All of the boys started to laugh at Omari as he stood there to take the laughter from the boys.

"I would have taken that to my grave," Quez said as he continued to laugh. "I mean this is not what you say to prove you're a bad man."

"Anyway, lets go Carter," Omari said as he started walking to the exit of the school, as Carter, Quez and Tommy started to follow.

"Where are you guys going," Tommy asked as everyone walked towards a a local transit bus stop.

"We are heading to the Alamodome to get Spurs tickets for tomorrows playoff game," Carter said.

"THE SPURS," Quez and Tommy yelled and started to laugh at the two friends.

"Man they going to get smoked by the Jazz," Tommy said.

"Well I love them and I want to take Carter to a game," Omari said as he turned around to see if the bus is coming.

Tommy and Quez started to look a little quizzical at the two and turned around to see if the bus is coming.

"Why are you guys going right now," Quez said. "Why can't you guys go after school or tomorrow at the box office."

"They think the game is going to be sold out and I have to go to dinner with my parents, sister and her boyfriend tonight so this is the only time I can be able to get the tickets," Omari said.

"What are you going to tell your parents when they find out you got tickets," Tommy asked.

"We won them in some contest," Carter said. "We thought of everything.

As the sun started to come out and shine brighter to start the day, the four teenagers stood and waited for the bus to come from down the street.

"Where are you guys planning on sitting at," Quez asked as he put his hands in his pocket and looked at Tommy.

"I think we will have to sit in "Mr. Robinson's neighorhood", because everyone thinks this is their year," Omari said. "Like I said, the game is going to be sold out."

"You guys do know the first two games in the series are going to be here," Tommy said. "I was watching the news and they said game two is going to be on Saturday afternoon."

"Yeah but we want to go to tomorrows game," Carter said as he pulled out his bus money. "Our first two periods can be made up later and we are going to turn in our homework by the end of the day. We thought about everything."

"How are you all going to tell your parents about missing the first two periods of," Quez asked.

"I will say we were working on my English report in the library," Carter said. "Mom knows I have been working on this paper for the past two days. She will believe that."

Quez looked at the two teens as if they are out of their minds but he shook his head at them in admiration.

"You guys are brave," Quez said as he pulled out some change from his pocket. "Do you guys mind me coming with you all? The Warriors are playing on Friday so I won't miss the game."

Everyone looked at Quez kind of weird. Omari and Carter then looked at each other and Carter shook his head in agreeance to letting him go.

"Yeah you can go," Carter said. "Why do you want to go? Won't you get in trouble with your coaches."

Quez started to adjust his backpack and look in his hand to count the change.

"Yeah but I never thought about going to a game until I heard you guys," Quez said. "This will be the first time I can go to a basketball game so why not go even though it is the sorry ass Spurs and the boring Jazz."

Tommy looked at them and everyone can tell he thought about going with the others.

"Quez I will see you during lunch," Tommy said. "I don't want to risk my parents finding out and getting in trouble."

"Cool bro," Quez said. "I'll get your geometry notes so I will not get behind."

Tommy and Quez gives eachother a bro hug then Tommy pulls a $20 bill out out of his wallet and gives it to his friend.

"If you get a ticket, get me one also," Tommy said. "If I use these guys excuse to getting a ticket, I think my parents will fall for it to."

As the bus pulled up to the bus stop, the three teens walk on it and sits on the back of the bus. Each of the teens got their own seat and rode the bus down the road when it stopped a little further down the street. This was when they saw Marlon getting on the bus.

"Hey bro whats going on," Carter asked. "You were able to get make it?"

Marlon started to walk to the back to talk to the teens and noticed Quez was with them.

"Yo whats up guys," Marlon said as he shook hands with Omari and Carter. Then turns and looks at Quez. "What's up Bitch?"

Quez stood up and was about to charge Marlon but Carter got in between the two.

"What the fuck did you just say?" Quez said in an angry tone.

"Just because we're on a bus don't mean I forgot what happened," Marlon said. "Then you call my girl a bitch."

"Cause the bitch is a bitch," Quez said as he got up from his bus seat and walked towards Marlon. Omari was able to get in between the two teenagers as they yelled at each other. The bus was not full but the patron who was on the bus watched them attempt to fight. As the bus driver pulled the bus to the side of the road, he got up and walked to them. The 6'4 hispanic man who looks like he weighed close to 300 lbs stood behind Marlon.

"I'm not gonna tell you no damn mo, sit yo ass down," the bus driver said in a deep stern tone. Marlon, Quez and Omari looked at the driver for a couple of seconds before sitting down in their seats. The driver walked back to the drivers seat and started to drive the bus.

"Just like daddy," Carter said as he laughed. "I felt that."

"I don't think I want to get off or I may get my ass whooped," Quez said as he started to laugh with Carter.

Omari and Marlon had could not hold it in and started to laugh. The teens imitated the bus driver as the rest of the bus riding patrons went a long with them. After half of the bus ride, the laughing went down to a chordal.

"Marlon, where are you going?" Carter asked. Marlon sat up from his bus seat and adjusted his cap.

"I was going to skip school," Marlon said. "My homeboy goes to Brack and just going to chill at his place. Why are you guys not at school?"

"We are getting playoff tickets," Carter said.

"For the Spurs and Jazz?" Marlon asked. "Why the hell are y'all going to the game?"

"This is the only time we can get the tickets," Omari said. "If we go now and get the tickets, we should be back by the middle of third period."

"Fuck the Spurs," Marlon said. "I like the Magic. Penny got skills. Jordan is lucky he retired cause he would have embarassed him."

"Only Hardaway who will embarass you is Tim," Quez said. "No one has handkles like Tim cause he has a habit of crossing people for a living. He is that good."

"What?", said Marlon said with a high voice. "Have you watched Penny play? "This dude can do the samething as Tim but he is taller than will bang on you. He is my favorite player."

"I like Shawn Kemp," said Carter. "Have you seen anyone trying to stop him when he has the ball?

The bus traveled all the way to the Alamodome and as the teens got off and were still talking about basketball all the way up to the ticket box. As the teens walked up the stairs, Carter stopped and grabbed his chest. Omari ran back down to help him up the stairs.

"Hey, what is wrong with," Marlon asked.

"Carter is fine," Omari said as he was slowly helping his friend up the stairs. "It is none of your business whais wrong. He will be ok."

"It became our business when it looks like he is about to die around us," Quez said. "What is wrong?"

Carter and Omari stop and look at each other and then Carter gives Omari a head nod.

"Technically, Carter is dieing," Omari said. "He has cancer and scoliosis we don't know when he is going to die. "

Quez and Marlon stood in shock as they look at Carter with pity. With Carter looking at them, he gets angry and slightly pushes Omari off of him.

"I know what you are thinking and about to say I'm sorry or I didn't know," Carter said in a stern voice. "My mom told me not to cry and feel sorry for me so I do not want your sympathy and pity. I am ok with this."

"This is why we are here," Omari said. "Carter has never been to a game and he wanted to go to an NBA game just in case the worst."

Omari then walked away for a moment to wipe the tears away and wiped the tears away from his eyes.

"No one knows this so, don't say anything," Carter said. "This would be one of my dieing wish."

Quez and Marlon still looking shocked at the two and then looked back at looked back at Carter as Omari walked back towards the group of guys.

"Alright," Marlon said. "I mean you still look like a Bruteman from the Thundercats."

The four teens start to laugh and then walk to the box office to get their tickets. After they got their tickets, they walked to the bus stop to catch a bus back to school and was able to make it back in time before the start of third period. During the seventh period athletics, Quez was in the locker room getting ready for practice in his gym shorts, shirt and shoes when on of the coaches approach him.

"Childress, what is going on?" the coach asked. "I got a notice for you to go to the office."

Quez has a skeptical look at his the coach as he stood up to look at the coach.

"I have no idea what is going on coach," Quez said. "I am sorry but I wish I can tell you what is going on."

"Go on to the office and come back as soon as possible," the coach said.

Quez walked out of the locker room and towards the schools main office. As he opened the door, Omari, Carter and Marlon are there.

"What the hell is going on here?" Quez whispered to the other teenagers.

"I don't know," Omari said. "I was told to come to the office."

"Me too," Marlon said.

Carter nodded his head to agree with everyone.

"I bet you it is about us missing the first two periods," Quez said as he sat down next to Marlon.

Right after Quez sat down, a short petite white woman with short blonde hair walks out of the office with named Yolanda Bennett. She looks around and see the teens and strolls towards them.

"Marquez Childress, Carter Johnson, Marlon Braxton and Omari James," the principal said to the four teens.

All four said yes ma'am. The principal then did a finger gesture to what looks like a conference room where all five of them walked into. As soon as they walked into the room, five adults were sitting down at the table.

"What the," Marlon said. "Dad what are you..."

Marlon was interupted by tall husky black man with a thick beard and glasses.

"Why the hell you going to the Alamodome," Marlon's father yelled.

As the four teens sat far away from their parents, the principal walked to the front of the conference table.

"Let's calm down for a moment," the principal said. "I wanted to bring you all in here because I wanted to get to the bottom of this and hope they do not make a habit of skipping school."

The five parents sat quiet but each one of them had a disappointing glare at the teenagers.

"I am just concerened because these four are model students and this does not seem like something they have done," the principal said. "Two of them are outstanding student athletes, while Omari and Carter's grades are off the chart. If there is something you want to talk to us about, let me know because I see a bright future with you four."

The tension in the room seemed to come down a little but it s obvious the parents are still not happy with being called to school.

"Omari, look at me," a lady said to him.

"Yes mom," Omari said as he had a hard time looking at his mother. "What is going on? Why were you downtown? Are you in a gang?"

At that moment all of the parents started to yell and jump on the four teens. While the principal had a hard time getting order back into the room, all four students sank lower into their seats. As everything got worse and worse, Quez stood up and walked to one set of parents.

"Mom, dad," Quez said. "Can I talk to you both outside?

Both Quez's mom who is about 5'3 petite woman and his 6'6 father stood up and followed their son outside the conference room while the other parents stopped and watched as they walked outside the door.

"Where are they going," Marlon's father surprisingly asked.

"I don't know what is going on but I want to know why you weren't at school Carter," A woman who sat down on at the corner of the table said with tears coming down her face.

"Mom, it isn't what you think," Carter said. "I just had something I needed to do."

As Carter's mom stood up her face went from scared to anger.

"What do you mean this is something you needed to do," Carter's mom said as if it was thunder in a bad thunderstorm.

Carter's mom is a short chubby lady stared at him with fire in her eyes and if it looks as if she is taking his soul as he sat down. At that moment, Quez and his parents walked back into the conference room.

"Quez take the four boys outside and sit down until we call you back in," Quez's father said to him in a calm voice.

The three boys got up and followed Quez out of the conference room and sat down where they were originally at.

"What did you say," Omari whispered to Quez.

"The right thing," Quez said as he looked forward and closed his eyes.

Carter got up from his chair and stood over Quez with his fist bald up.

"Don't tell me you told your parents about me," Carter said angrily. "I told you not to tell anyone. My mother has too much going on for everyone to know our business. Fuck you man. Fuck you."

Marlon stood up to have Carter sit down in his chair.

"Quez that was fucked up of you man," Marlon said as he walked back to his seat.

The principal opened the conference door and asked for the teenagers to come back in. Quez was the first one to get up and go into the conference room while the other three gingerly walked in. As they entered the conference room, Carter's mom was crying and being consoled by a crying Omari and Quez's mom. Marlon's dad walks up to his son and hugged him and the principal had tears coming down her face with a smile when he saw the four boys.

"I wish I had four friends like you," the principal said as she wiped the tears from her eyes.

The four boys looked surprised surprised at what is going on.

"You boys have made my day," Carter's mom said as she cries. "This let me know everything is going to be alright."

As Quez and Omari sat down in their original spot, Carter walked to his mother and hugged her. Marlon let go from his father's embrace and walked closer to Carter's mom.

"I am sorry ma'am but what is going on," Marlon asked as he kneeled next to the crying mother.

"Quez told us why you all missed the first two periods and I think this is admirable," the principal said as she continued to smile. "You all went risked everything for a friends last wish. I understand.

Quez's dad walks up to him and reaches out to shake his hand.

"Son, I would be pissed at you but right now, I actually admire you for doing this," Quez's dad said.

"Dad it was actually Omari's idea," Quez said as he looked at Omari. "I just happened to go along for the ride."

Carter's mom stood up and walks up to Omari and hugs him.

"I had a feeling you did," Carter's mom said. "Thank you so much for being a great friend for my son."

Quez's voice:

This was the start of a meaningful friendship with us. We didn't get in trouble that day because the principal didn't have it in her heart to suspend us or send us to ISS because of what we did for Carter. It was a good thing Tommy did not go with us to the Alamodome. I have known him since kindergarten and his parents are not understanding when it comes to school and friendship. I told my parents because mom is a Grief Counselor and dad is an Oncologist and I felt they would have been able to help Carter and his family through these tough times. The next night Marlon's and my father took all five of us to the game where we sat in the top row or "Mr. Robinson's neighborhood". The Spurs beat the Jazz 106-89 to take the first game of a best of three series and all five of us had the time of our life. Omari's dad happened to know someone who worked for the team and was able to get us on the floor after the game and we met Dennis Rodman and Omari's favorite player Negele Knight. Carter told us he had two years to live but apparently this inspired him to find a way to keep on living and find every way to fight this disease. Because of my budding friendship with Marlon, I overlooked my crush with Macy and from that day forward. You would not believed how we pushed each other through high school and college to be a better student athlete. We did get punished though. Our parents made us go with Carter to all of his chemo therapy. I am not a Spur's fan but watching Carter enjoy this moment made almost fighting Marlon, missing school to hang out with those three jokers, and getting yelled at worth that moment and it all started with skipping school and snitching on my friend.

In the present times

Quez and Marlon laugh uncontrollable and put their hands on each others shoulders.

"I always wanted to know but did your dad whoop your ass," Quez asked.

"Hell yeah," Marlon responded. "He thought I was admirable and all that good shit. He was pissed I skipped classes and almost messed up a chance at a scholarship. What about you?"

Quez turned and looked at Marlon, and his eyes widen.

"You been around my dad for over 20 years," Quez said as both friends started to laugh. "You should know that answer. I was going to take this to my grave."

As a gentle breeze touched the two friends. Quez closes his eyes and smiled.

"Darwin Childress was no joke," Marlon said. "He probably took you to the boxing mat when we left school didn't he?

Quez nodded his head yes as to answer Marlon's question.

"Remember when he wanted to box us both for coming in late from the movie," Marlon said. "Shit, my dad told him to knock me out because he couldn't get to me."

Quez opened his eyes in shock and turned around to look at Marlon.

"Are you serious," Quez said. "I remember dad wanting to beat us but didn't know your dad ok'd it."

"Better your dad than mine," Marlon said in a high pitched tone. "Shit, I would take going to the mat with your dad any day than getting my ass whooped by mine."

The two friends let out another chuckle, then turned around to look at Carter's head stone. There the two friends would be silent for a moment and hear nothing around them but another gentle breeze would touch them. Quez let out a sigh while Marlon started to get antsy around the grave site.

"Are you still nervous about being out here," Quez asked when he opened his eyes.

"No fool," Marlon said. "I got to pee. I should have went before I drove out here."

Quez shooked his head at Marlon.

"I think they have a restroom in the building. Go on and go and I will wait for you by the cars," Quez said.

As Marlon walked off to the restroom, Quez turned and kneeled to Carter's headstone while touching it.

"I love you brother," Quez whispered. "You are an inspiration to me and the glue to the brotherhood. Thank you for all that you have done being there for me."

Quez walk to his car and a filipino man gets out of a blue sports car that was parked next to his.

"Tommy," Quez said as he walked to his old friend and gave him a bro hug. "How long have you been here."

"I was about to leave when I saw you pull up," Tommy said. "I just waited for you to finish talking to Carter. Where did Marlon go?"

"He had to piss," Quez said while smiling at his old friend. "You know that fool doesn't have his priorities together."

The two start to laugh and walk towards the building where Marlon was at.

"When did you get into town," Tommy asked as he put on his sun glasses.

"Just did," Quez said. "I wanted to see him before I called everyone. I got to see mom's before I do anything tonight."

"I know bro," Tommy said as he put his arms around Quez and brought him in closer. "I am just glad you are in town. I miss you bro."

"I miss you all too," Quez said.

As the two friends walked to the cemetary's main office building, Marlon was walking out.

"Hey Tommy," Marlon said as he walked up and gave him a bro hug. "You got here quick. I take it you were speed racer huh."

As the three old friends circled around eachother, Marlon took off his glasses off and put on his shades.

"Man, I told you I was on my way while you were walking up to Carter's grave," Tommy said as he let out a laugh. "I just wanted to fuck with you."

"He means he was stalking us both," Quez said as he laughed back. "You know how he is. Always trying to sneak up on people."

Tommy shook his head and smiled.

"Yeah you know me," Tommy said. "Always sneaking up on people. I even know what you did last night. Keep it up and I will tell everyone what you are up to."

"I don't think everyone wants to hear about a former star athlete who is a family man who spends his days scratching himself," Marlon said.

"You mean a champion family man scratching himself," Quez said. "I think you are still news bro but Macy won't let you do anything."

"Man, I am surprised your wife let you out of the house," Tommy said. "It takes an act of God just for him to come out with us."

"She don't know I am with you all," Marlon said as he let out a chuckle. "She thinks I am getting a loaf of bread.

"She got you in check," Tommy said.

"Oh I am sorry Mr. Ibanez," Marlon said snidely. "Do you think when you marry Jenny, you are going to run around all willie nillie? Shit, you going to be lucky to keep your baby."

Marlon points to Tommy's sports car and Quez has a quizzical look.

"Is there something I need to know," Quez said.

"Man shut the fuck up," Tommy said.

With the sun leaning on the three friends, they start to walk back to the parking lot from the building.

"I am glad I don't live in Texas anymore," Quez said as he wiped the sweat from his forehead. "Damn it's hot."

"Well we have to live with it," Tommy said as he did the same. "I was about to go to Omari's before we go and get something to eat. You all want to come.

"I was thinking the samething," Marlon said. "I don't know why but remember how it took us all night just to get something to eat."

The three friends laughed and got in their cars.

We ain't never going to get anything to eat!

Summer 1998

Quez's voice:

After graduating from high school, all of us went off to college. Since Marlon, Tommy and I are a year older, we took Omari and Craig out on a night on the town their graduation night. Omari and I went to the University of Houston. My football career allowed me to play wide receiver for the Cougars and get my bachelors in Communications while Omari was attending before he goes to law school to be an attorney. Marlon's high school basketball career sent him to Tulsa, where he played basketball and get his degree in Business Degree. Tommy stayed in town but attended the University of Texas in hope he to becoming a doctor. As for Carter, because of his cancer and he didn't want to move far away from his doctors and treatments, he stayed home to University of Texas at San Antonio to get his degree in engineering. Because I was surprise player of the year I was like the big man on campus. Marlon on the other hand has been all over magazines and the talk of sports shows. Hell, there was a mock draft that had my friend playing for the Nets. We both made a promise to our parents we were going to get our education before thinking pro. Tommy spends most of his times getting every advantage to get into med school and Carter.... Well he wants to design an underground tramway from San Antonio to Killeen. Distance has not weakened our friendship because we use email to stay in touch but since Omari and I go to the same school, our friendship got a lot closer than the others. We helped each other through all the trying times that a young adult would go through outside of school. The Summer of 98 was a turning point for us , and it started on a June night. Carter asks us all to come over so we can run to IHOP to get something to eat. Normally I would drive but

Omari's parents got him a new Toyota sedan and he said he would pick up me, Marlon and Tommy. Five years from the first time we all started to hang out with each other, we look the same but when I see babyface Omari have facial hair and Marlon get a tattoe, I see we are getting older. I sat in the passenger seat and put on the Makaveli CD as we started to ride to Carter's house.

10:30 p.m.

"Hey, put on Just like daddy," Marlon said. "That's my song."

Quez put the cd on the song, and Omari looked at him kind of crazy.

"Hey what makes you think I want to listen to this," Omari said. "You know how much of an asshole you are when it comes to your stereo. It's payback motherfucker."

Everyone starts to laugh and tease Quez.

"Tommy I know you ain't got shit to say," Quez said. "Everytime we ride with you, we listen to love songs like you are serenading us."

"And you know when you are in my car, you're going to listen to what I want," Tommy said.

"Negro, Shut your ass up," Quez said as he chuckled. "You should know the main rule. Never listen to love songs with a group of men."

"Yeah Tommy, you should know that rule," Marlon said. "The only reason why I ride with you is to get to point B. I feel like you expect me to kiss you when you take me home."

"Why the fuck are you thinking about that," Tommy shockingly asked. "Are you gay?"

"You're Gay," Marlon, Quez and Omari said at the sametime as they laughed at.

"Fuck you guys," Tommy said as he chuckled. "I ain't gay. I love pussy and pussy loves me."

Quez turned around and looked at two guys in the back seat while everyone was laughing.

"All jokes aside," Quez said. "Guess who I saw when I walking around the mall today."

"Who," Tommy, Omari and Marlon asked

"Macy Bennett," Quez said as he looks at Marlon. "She asked if I heard from you."

Marlon's had a surprise look on his face and sat up from the backseat of the car.

"What did you say," Marlon said. "I tried to reach out to her last year but her dad said she was dating some guy."

"Yeah she was dating some guy who is a manager at a car company," Omari said. "She swore up and down she wanted to get back together with you but this guy came around and took her on some dates."

"I told her I was going to see you tonight and let you know she asked about you," Quez said.

"Hold up Q," Marlon said as he started to raise his voice. "Why didn't you tell me she wanted to get back with me but she was dating some guy."

"When you two broke up, you said I don't want to hear from her or know what is going on," Omari said as he kept his eyes on the road. "I am not getting in the middle of this love spat with you guys."

"But you could have told me," Marlon said.

"I could have but again you said, don't want to know anything about Macy," Omari said. "Make up your damn mind. Do you want to know what is going on with her or not?"

Marlon sat back in his seat and the color on his face drained. Quez and Tommy looked at Tommy with concern with their friend.

"She said you can call her," Quez said. "When we get to Carter's, why don't you call her. She is going to be home all night."

As Marlon stared out of the backseat window into the night sky, Tommy shrugs at Quez. Quez turns back around and touches the radio. Omari slaps Quez's hand like if he was reaching into the cookie jar. Quez grabbed his and scowled with Omari.

"I told you don't touch my radio," Omari said with a grin on his face.

The boys pull up to the side of a one story home in a nice quiet neighborhood. The porch lights off illuminated the dark street made it hard for the boys to walk from the street to the Carter's door.

"Why the hell didn't he turn on the porch light," Quez said with a raised voice.

"Keep your voice down," Tommy said. "You know Carter's mom is probably a sleep and you know we do not want to wake her up."

As they got to the door, Carter opened it to greet his long time friends.

"Damn, took yall long enough," Carter said. "I was starving my ass off."

As the four friends walk in the house, they each gave Carter a bro hug.

"Shut yo ass up," Quez said. "We are going to IHOP, not Pancho's."

Quez turned around and saw two young ladies about the same age as themsitting at the table.

"Oh shit," Quez said with a surprise look on his face. "Who are they?"

"Oh yeah, this is my cousin Stephanie and her friend Gina," Carter said as he closed the door

As Stephanie stood up, her short stature, light brown skin and curly hair owned the room. Since it was summer time, she wore short blue jean shorts and a tank top. Stephanie was followed by Gina is a tall athletic hispanic young lady who wore athletic shorts and a t-shirt and smiled as she followed her friend.

"Hi guys," Gina said as she shook everyone's hand with her smile. "You must be Quez. I saw you play against Tulane last year. What was your stats?"

"I finished with 7 receptions for 78 yards and two touchdowns," I was surprised about the second."

"I wasn't," Gina said. "Carter brags about how good you are. He even has us watching your game also."

Gina turns to Marlon and shakes his hand as she blushes.

"If you make it to the NBA, can you get me tickets," Gina asked as the two young ladies walked back to the dining which their young developed bodies got the attention of the fellas. Carter hit Quez on the shoulder when he saw Quez smile at them.

"Bro what the fuck," Carter whispered to Quez.

"Your cousin got an ass on her," Quez said with a smile.

The girls walked back to the dining room table and it is safe to As the fellas sat down on the couch, Carter walked down the hallway into his bedroom. For a moment, silence fell into living room area while everyone stared at each other.

"Stephanie, you look familiar," Omari asked as he sat up to look at her. "Where have I known you from?"

Stephanie smiled at him and blushed.

"Yes you did," Stephanie said. "We met at the family reunion."

Omari's eyes widen as stood up.

"Oh shit," Omari said. "You said your name was Tiffany. You lied to me"

Stephanie continued to smile at Omari and sat up.

"When I was younger, I went by my middle name Tiffany," Stephanie said. "I didn't lie to you."

Omari stood up and walked to the dining room table and sat down next to Stephanie.

"Well hell, you grew up," Omari said. "Why are you guys here?"

"Gina and I just graduated from high school and was going to Dallas for our graduation present," Stephanie said. "We decided to see Carter before we hit the road. Especially since you all are going to IHOP."

Marlon sat up from the couch and started to laugh.

"Hold up," Marlon said as he stood up and looked in the girls direction. "You gave him a fake name.

"Yeah, all that I heard was you duped my boy," Tommy said with a chuckle.

As the young adults started to laugh, Carter's mom came from her room and into the living room.

"She was scared to talk to you," Carter's mom said as she walked to the refrigerator to get a soda and walked back to her bedroom. "Everytime we are at a family gathering she asks how you are doing. It was annoying me."

Stephanie covered her face so no one can see her blush while Gina grabbed her hand. Carter walked out of his bedroom and sat next to Tommy.

"I thought you had a girlfriend," Stephanie said as she reached out for Omari's hand.

"What are you talking about," Omari said with a puzzled look on his face. "I haven't even gone on a date yet."

"I wouldn't have said that out loud," Tommy said while chuckling.

"You said you were going to dinner with this girl named Maggie or Marley," Stephanie said.

"You mean Maddie," Omari said as he placed his other hand on top of hers. "My sister's name is Madeline and we call her Maddie. She was going off to college and wanted to take me out before she left"

Stephanie slowly moved her hand from eyes and the two smiled at each other. Tommy and Quez looked at the two and made an approval look to each other.

"Are we going to eat something or what," Carter asked as he was putting on his shoes.

Marlon got up from the couch and picked up the phone as Gina got up and head to the living room.

"Yeah, I am hungry," Gina said as she rubbed her stomach. "I haven't eaten since earlier today."

Tommy, Quez and Carter followed Gina outside as Omari and Stephanie slowly got up from the table to follow them. Marlon made a phone call.

"Hey Macy," Marlon said softly. "Quez told me you wanted me to call you."

As he backed up against the wall, he slouched down to sit down on the floor.

"I know you have been watching my games," Marlon said with a smile. "Did you do my sign when I made the game winner against the Cowboys? I think about you all the time. Do you think about me?"

While Marlon was on the phone talking to Macy, the others were outside by the cars waiting on him. Omari and Stephanie stood by the driver side. Even though it was dark outside, the two were not able to keep their eyes off each other.

"I thought about you and wondered how you were doing," Omari said softly to Stephanie. "I wish you would hve called.

"Well how come you never asked about me," Stephanie said in a softly. "You know it goes two ways."

Omari closed his eyes for a moment and then opened them to look in Stephanie's eyes. Omari grabbed Stephanie's hand and brought her closer to him.

"I wanted to but your brother looked at me like he wanted to hit me," Omari said with tears coming from his eyes. "I didn't know what to do."

Stephanie smiled and slowly got closer to Omari.

"Don't worry about him," Stephanie said as she put her arms around Omari's waist. "He has no say so as to what I do or who I am I with."

With Omari's tall stature, he put his arms around Stephanie's neck where the two slowly reached in for a long passionate kiss.

"What the hell," Quez said shockingly. "You guys just met back up in what six years and you got her like that. Do Omari got game like that?"

"I guess so," Gina said. "She has been my homegirl since kindergarten and I never knew I never knew anyone to sweep her off her feet like that."

As the friends walk away to give Stephanie and Omari a moment alone, Marlon walks out of the house to catch up with them.

"Yo, is Mari getting with ol girl," Marlon shockingly said as he ran up to the group.

"I had a feeling this was going to happen," Carter said.

"How did you know this was going to happen," Marlon said.

"You called Macy huh," Tommy said.

"Yeah," Tommy said as he was catching his breath. "She wanted to know how I am doing. I might as well see whats up?"

Quez and Tommy gave Marlon a weird gaze.

"You miss her," Carter said. "We already know. You're a big man on campus and didn't fuck anyone. We already know."

"So what if I do," Marlon said. "At least I won't be the only one who may have a girl. Look at Omari and ol girl. He got the magic touch in less than five minutes."

Gina laughed while Quez shook his head.

"Every since they met each other, all they do is ask about each other," Carter said. "It started to get annoying."

"I remember when she called me and talked my ear off about him," Gina said. "I thought he was made up. She didn't even date someone."

Quez stopped walking.

"What?" Quez asked. "Are you serious?"

Gina turned around and walked back to Quez with the others following.

"Yes, Stephanie hasn't dated anyone," Gina said. "Her mom didn't want her to date anyone until she graduated from high school."

"So Gina, are you seeing anyone?" Tommy asked. "I am asking just in case if anyone wants to hit on you."

Gina turns away from the group so no one can see her blush.

"I have a boyfriend guys," Gina said as she chuckled. "I have been with Donald for two years."

"Why isn't he going with you to Dallas?" Quez asked as he walked up to Gina. "Do he trust you like that?"

"He is in the Army and stationed in North Carolina," Gina said. "I am moving up there in July. I think he wants to marry me."

"I am going to be the best man in their wedding," Carter said. "Donald said he wants me at his wedding just in case the worst happens."

"Guys, I think we may want to make sure Omari isn't trying to fuck Stephanie," Quez said.

"What makes you think he would," Tommy said as he turn to look at Quez. "Omari is a good guy."

"Cause he is a guy who just got a taste of a female," Quez said as he walked up to stare at his friend in the eyes. The two stood face to face for a couple of seconds until Tommy raised his eyebrow.

"Uh huh," Quez said.

Marlon started to run back to the house as the others followed. As they got back, Omari had Stephanie wrapped around his arms as they both had a smile on their face and looking to the night sky.

"Hey!" Marlon yelled "Is this foreal or are you two just happy to see eachother,"

"I think both," Stephanie said while she looked at Omari with love in her eyes.

"Are we going to get something to eat?" Carter asked while he was walking up to the group.

"We are but the girls have to go and get ready to for their road trip," Omari said while he was looking Stephanie. "She told me she hasn't packed for Dallas."

Stephanie's face looked destroyed until Omari touched her chin and kissed her.

"Call me when you are about to leave," Omari said. "I will wake up early and wait for you."

"Do you promise," Stephanie asked in a whisper.

"The same as I waited for you to call me six years ago," Omari said as he reached down and kissed her.

"I wanted some damn pancakes and an omlet," Gina said as if she was a five year old wanting ice cream. "Why didn't you pack?

Quez walks up to Gina and grabbed her arm.

"Don't call me when you leave cause I am going to be asleep," Quez said as he was mocking Omari. "Now take your fine ass and get in the car. I don't think I will see you ever again."

Gina laughs at Quez as she walks to the car.

"I read up on you and Marlon," Gina said. "He is going to be drafted so I think I will be seeing you all from this point on. Especially if they get together."

"Good luck on getting with him, " Quez said while pointing at Marlon. "He just called his ex-girlfriend and I think she is trying to get back with him."

Quez opened the driver side car door for Gina while Stephanie gets in the passenger side. As Stephanie gets in the car, Omari leans in and kisses her.

"Let's do this right," Omari whispers to her with a smile.

Stephanie shook her head as she smiled. Gina started to car and the girls drove off, the fellas watched the car go down the street until the darkness swallowed it up. With the girls down the road, the fellas stare at Omari.

"What?" Omari asked.

"You got a gift," Quez said. "You got to teach me about the game ol wise one."

"Oh yes, please teach us the game," Tommy said as he bowed towards Omari. "I humbley beg of you."

The fellas laugh at Omari as they walk to the car so they can make their journey into the night.

12:01 a.m.

The boys pulled into the parking lot a popular hang out spot named Diversions Gameroom. Dozens of young adults pour in and out of the building as some by their cars and talk to each other.

"Man why the fuck are we here," Marlon wined. "I am fuckin hungry."

"I owe Quez an asswhoopin at NBA James," Omari said. "IHOP is 24 hours and down the street. It ain't going no where. Plus wouldn't you want to see your fans.

As the fellas get out of the car to go into the gameroom, Marlon attracts a couple of fans. He stops to talk to them, while the others went in to play some games. Carter went over to the Super Street Fighter II video game that had a lot of people waiting for their turn to play the winner of the game. Tommy, Quez and Omari walked to an empty NBA Jams game where they decided to play where the two friends played and the other watched. During the game, a group of five young men walk up to watch them play the game.

"Whats up Tommy?" said one of the young men in a booming deep voice. "Where have you been hiding?"

As Tommy turned around from watching the game to see a tall hispanic male.

"Johnny!" Tommy said with excitement in his voice and reached out to give him a bro hug. "What have you been doing?

Tommy looks over his friends shoulder and see the other young men standing behind Johnny.

"Whats up, T.A., Chance, Dyson, Rock," Tommy said as he reaches out to bro hugs each of them. "What have you guys been up to?"

"Aw man, we are just chillin," one of the taller black males said. "I am working at this call center.

"Thats all gravy, Dyson," Tommy said. "Where have you been bro? I haven't seen you since graduation.

"I go to UT trying to get into med school," Tommy said. "I barely make it back. Man y'all can come up and visit. Quez and Omari do.

The others start to laugh at Tommy.

"That's some gay shit man," one of the short fat black guys said. "I ain't going up to Austin to visit no man."

Tommy stares at the guy.

"TA, you hang out with a bunch of guys," Tommy said. "Is that gay too or just because you travel to see a friend?

Quez and Omari walks up to group after their game and shook hands with everyone.

"Whats up Quez?" Johnny said. "I saw your game against Tulane. Man I knew you would act a fool."

Quez has a smirk on his face and raised his arms in amazement.

"Was anyone surprised?" Quez said as if he was grandstanding in front of people. "Those fools had no answer for me. We open the season against Mizzu and I can't wait to show everyone my coming out party. Who wants an autograph?"

Everyone starts to laugh.

"Shit, I want one," Johnny said. "If you get famous, I want to tell everyone I went to school with you. How much pussy do you get on campus?"

"I get some on a regular," Quez said. "Hell these broads love giving it up."

"Hook me up," TA said.

"Alright man," Quez said. "I got you.

"You ain't getting as much as TA," one of the fellas said. "He gets it all the time and has two babies and one on the way."

Omari and Tommy has a shock look on their faces as they stare at TA.

"The fuck," Tommy said with a hyper tone. "Aren't you like 19?

"Yeah, but you know how it is," TA said. "I be fuckin though. I have two one-year old daughters.

Omari leaned into Tommy

"What an example to your kids," Omari whispered into Tommy's ear.

"Oh damn bro," Quez said as his eyes got wide. "I guess you got game huh."

"What are you all getting into?" Johnny asked. "We are about to heading to Janie Montgomery's house. She told Dyson her friends are there with some drank. Y'all should come through."

"I think we are just going to head to IHOP and then go home bro," Quez said. "But we may head that way when we are done."

Omari looked at Quez while Tommy did a facepalm.

"What?" Quez asked.

Johnny and the group of young men walk to another videogame as two of them played Killer Instict 2 while Tommy and Omari smacked Quez across the head

"We ain't going over there," Omari said in a stern voice. "We are going to head to IHOP and then go home. Don't be stupid man. Janie and her skanky friends will ruin everything man."

"What the fuck ever man," Quez said as he walked away from the two friends and stormed out of the arcade. Marlon who was still outside talking to some of his fans, ran after Quez.

"What's going on man?" Marlon asked while running up to Quez. "Where are you going?"

"Your boy is pissing me off," Quez said. "He trying to dictate where we are going and what to do. Like he is someones daddy. Who named his leader of our crew?"

Marlon grabbed Quez's shoulder to stop him from walking.

"What are you talking about?" Marlon asked.

Quez looks at Marlon for a moment and then started to pace back and forth.

"You remember Johnny Vargas," Quez said. He was telling us about coming through to Janie Montgomery's house because a couple of her friends were going to be there. Man I want to get my dick sucked."

Marlon looked at the Quez and stopped him from pacing.

"I wan't you to think long and hard," Marlon said as he looked Quez in the eyes. "If Omari said this, then he did for a reason. Think about this man. We are college athletes who are about to make it man. We don't need shit like this man. Any party or people Johnny Vargas and his friends go to is not a place we should go. Especially getting your dick sucked."

The look on Quez start to come down from his anger.

"Bro, for five years it has been us," Marlon said. "We have looked out for each other from Carter's still being a live despite being told he was supposed to be dead. Our games, Tommy being valedictorian and Omari's first girl. Quez, this is about all of us. I never thought I was have any good friends like you. Especially after the basketball incident. I was like fuck you but if anyone fucks with you, they fuck with me. I just want to make sure you don't fall into anything stupid. That is not the way."

"I got you bro," Quez said as he reached out and gave Marlon a bro hug. "Do you know why I was mad at you?

"We all know you had a crush on Macy bro." Marlon said as he chuckled. "She knew it, I knew it, her friends and even your mom did. You should have found a better way to hide it."

While they were finish their talk, Carter, Omari and Tommy walks to their two friends.

"Are you ok?" Carter asked. "Cause I want some IHOP. Plus is it me or does it seem like Johnny and his boys are up to something?"

"I thought the samething," Omari said. "That's why we are going to get something to eat."

As the fellas start to walk to the car, they looked over and saw Johnny and his friends get in their car. Quez stops everyone in the middle of the parking lot.

"Let's wait for them to leave and then lets head out," Quez said. The rest of the group nodded as they watched the car full of the young men leave the Diversion's parking lot.

1:20 a.m.

As the fellas walk to Omari's car, a red sedan drove towards them before stopping next to them. A short young black lady jumps out of the driver side who run towards the group.

"Marlon!" she said as embraced him. "I couldn't wait for you to call me."

As the fellas stares at the two, Marlon puts his arms around her and buries her head in his chest.

"Macy, what are you doing here," Marlon said in a soft voice. As the sweat came down Macy's brow infused with her tears as she smiled at her high school love.

"I couldn't wait to see you," Macy said while Marlon wipes the tears from her eyes. Marlon's face went from happy to anger as he pulled away from Macy.

"But you are dating some guy huh," Marlon said in a soft but angry tone. Macy had a surprise look on her face as she turned and looked at Quez. While there is nothing Quez could do but shake his head and shrug hsi shoulder, Macy turned back and looked at Marlon.

"We broke up Marlon," Macy said as she was holding back tears. "For two years I waited for you to call but you never did. I guess being a superstar has you forgetting about me."

Marlon stood back and looked at her with an evil look.

"Forget about you?", Marlon asked. "Waited for you. What the hell are you talking about? You broke up with me. If I recall, you broke up with me because I chose Tulsa and not stay in Texas. What the hell do you want from me?"

"I want you to fight for me," Macy said as she started to cry. "I wanted you to stay with me always and not live without me."

"We ain't never going to get anything to eat!" Carter yelled as he dropped to his knees. Tommy, Quez and Omari start to walk towards the car and lean on the passenger side.

"You are so freakin selfish," Marlon said as he walked towards Macy. "You wanted me to drop my dreams for you. Is that what you want?"

"Yes," Macy said as she walked towards Marlon. "You are supposed to make me happy. That is what a man is supposed to do. Happy wife, happy life."

Marlon backed away from Macy and started to pace back and forth.

"You expected me to stop my dreams and do whatever you want," Marlon said with venom in his voice. "You want me to play basketball where you want me to just so you can be happy. Who told you what a man is supposed to do?"

"Mom told me what a man is supposed to do," Macy said. "If a man is wanting to marry a woman, he is supposed to make a woman happy by doing everything she wants."

"Wrong," Marlon said.

"We talked about marriage and you are supposed to make me happy," Macy said. "You would spend time with these guys all the time and

"Wrong," Marlon said.

"Instead of making me happy, you left me and left me alone," Macy said.

"Wrong!" Marlon yelled. "That is not what a relationship or marriage is. We are supposed to grow together and make each other happy not you. You're damn right, I hung out with my friends all the time. So fuckin what. They are my homeboys. You out of all people know everything we been through. How dare you? You're listening to single woman and watching trashy TV shows. I have a life and I am going to live it."

Tommy, Carter, Quez and Omari start to walk away so the former high school lovers can have a moment.

"No," Macy said. "You guys stay. I want you to hear how mean your friend is to me."

As the fellas stop, Quez walks towards to the two love birds.

"Mean to you," Quez said. "Cause he isn't kissing your ass and doing what you say is being mean. When you said he was mean to you, I didn't know it was this I am everywoman bs. I told Marlon I was going to stay out of it but this is the reason why you guys broke up, then my boy deserves someone better. Lets go fellas."

The fellas walk back into Diversions to let the two have a moment a lone.

"I am so fuckin hungry!" Carter wined as he walked through the door. Marlon walked over to Macy and grabbed her hands.

"Do not ever tell me what a man is supposed to do," Marlon said. "Last I recalled, you are not one so you can't tell me what a man is supposed to do. Making your sig other happy is one thing but the main thing a man is supposed to do is to take care of you. I am still learning what it takes to be one but damn it I have my dad who is helping me. Shiite Quez and Omari's dad also have put their foot in my ass if dad wasn't able to. So don't tell me what a man is supposed to do."

Macy continues to cry as she walked away while Marlon watched her get into her car. Macy sat down for a moment and then she got out of the car and stood in the front.

"Marlon, I love you," Macy said. "I just want you in my life. I will do whatever it takes to make it work. I just want you."

"If you want to be with me then you have to get out of this stupid way of thinking," Marlon said. "I am not your servant. I refuse to be with someone who thinks a man is some dumb idiot and just to be at your becon call."

Macy ran over to Marlon and hugs him and then kiss.

"Now go on home," Marlon said. "Carter is hungry, and we were supposed to get him something to eat. If we keep waiting then I'll have to pay for it. I will call you in the morning and we can finish this."

1:50 a.m.

After Marlon walked Macy to her car and watches her drive off, the fellas would get walk to their friend.

"Are you ok bro?" Tommy asked

"Yeah man," Marlon said as he looks up at the moon and then turned and looked at everyone. "This is a good night guys. Let's walk to IHOP."

Carter huffed and hunches over and starts to walk with his friends down the street towards the 24 restaraunt.

"Do you think she wants you because you're a hot comodity," Omari said. "I think she would run through all of your money before you signed your rookie contract."

"Naww," Marlon said. "If there is one thing about Macy, she isn't about money. She actually love me. I don't think I want to get married."

"Well, if you did get married, where would you want the wedding at?" Tommy asked as he jumped on Marlon's back.

"The real question is do we start planning Omari's wedding?" Carter asked. "I am glad those two finally got together." Omari looks away and start to blush at

"So she was the one you kept talking about?" Quez asked as he chuckled. "Where the fuck did that come from Mari? It is like you walked in, pointed your finger and said your my girl."

The boys laughed at the joke while Omari showed he was bashful.

"She almost got away," Omari said. "When I met her, it was at Carter's Family cook out. I was going into my freshman year of high school and this young lady who is two years younger than me kept hanging out with us. We played basketball and danced together.

"Everyone saw they were good together," Carter said. "But tonight, I did not see this coming. I thought they were going to have sex."

"Do we need to give her a pregnancy test?" Quez asked.

"They didn't have time to fuck," Tommy said to Quez.

"How long does it take for a woman to get pregnant Dr. Banaag?" Quez said as he looks at Tommy. Tommy and Quez does their normal stare at each other until the Tommy raises an eyebrow. "Yeah, yeah. Use the big doctor brain Dr. Banaag."

"Shut up," Tommy said as he laughed. "Just remember that when you decide to go to a house party and those hoochies try to get pregnant by you."

"I been telling him he needs to worry more about playing and stop sleeping with all these broads," Omari said. "There are some sexy ass broads on campus and he is like a big man on campus but leave those sluts alone."

"Bro, imagine telling ol Darwin you got some random broad pregnant," Marlon said. "I think your NFL career would end."

"I don't think his dad would kill him," Carter said. "He will need all the money to take care of that kid. If you get someone preggo can I be the God Father?"

"I ain't having no kids," Quez said. "Fuck that shit."

"Think about that the next time Nina comes to the dorm after a game," Omari said. "All she wants is to get you pregnant. Stop it or you going to be like TA with all these kids."

"I thought about that when he was telling us how many kids he has," Quez said. "Don't get me wrong, I love pussy but I got to protect myself."

"You mean putting on rubbers dumb ass," Tommy and Marlon said at the sametime. Quez, Carter and Omari started to laugh and then the other two started to chuckle with them. Even though it is a busy street, not one car was seen driving on this summer night as the fellas were able to cross the empty street to get to the other side. Majority of the stores on the strip are closed at the midnight hour but their signs illuminated the night sky. Silence takes over as the fellas walk towards the restaraunt.

"Come with me and the time we bump, dedicating slow jams on the radio," Quez said as he started to rap the lyrics to Just like Daddy. "I know your happy I can feel the passion looking out for ya just like daddy come on."

"Sunshine turns to rain baby I could take away your pain if you trust me," Everyone said as they joined in with Quez. "Close your eyes I can feel the magic never leave when you need me I do ya just like daddy."

"I met her when she was younger when her daddy died when she was younger," Carter said as he started to rap the song. "Her moms let her do what she please they said no one loved her. Her eyes shined love a diamond and above The kind that you can love

not yet touched with so much, potential. Youngster let me got ya mental and to a place

with a sourness of pain you'll never taste by God's grace. You were born with that face

Nothing but pure beauty. So for an eternity I feel it's my duty, to be a soldier. Dipping I got plans to mold ya and in the coldest nights is when I hold ya. Like I am suppose to, as we roll closer. I'll take your hand gladly, anything ya need ask me supporting my baby just like daddy.

"You alleviate tha stress spend time with you, I feel blessed," Tommy said as he rapped the next verse. "When you gone feel the pain so strong deep in my chest When I got arrested, came so close to going to jail Throwing blows at the po pos breaking they nails Screaming loud going all out Damn I did You stayed locked down at moms house Watching tha kids, through tha whole bid In the V-I I seen ya daily."

"When my fake homies try ta fuck you, you run and tell me," Omari said as he took over the rap verse. "That's why I stay committed, I thank God every time I hit it Hoping you'll forgive me for the times I bullshitted Me and you against the world We untouchable, screaming like ya dyin every time I'm fucking you. Ya never had a father or a family, but I'll be there. No need to fear so much insanity and through the years I know ya gave me your heart and plus when I am dirt broke and fucked up Ya still love me."

"Come with me and the time we bump, dedicate slow jams on the radio," All of the fellas said as they rapped the verse to the song. "I Know ya happy I can feel ya passion looking out foe ya just like daddy. Come on, sun shine turn to rain, baby I can take away ya pain if ya trust me close ya eyes feel the magic never leave when ya need me I do ya just like daddy."

"Boo would ya die for me?" Quez said as he started to rap the song. "Down holding my pistol, getting high with mean sounds tougher than brisles. Fool when you cry I'll be ya tissue back in the county writing letters how I miss you givin' you credit, apologetic how I dis you. Get you for thinking like a minor and on a level and sometime daddy ready to wine ya and dilain for total and twine ya. We right behind ya true Life just me and you no telling what we could do Getting high between the sheets Make the shit right here discrete Putting Nikes on ya belly while we fucking on the beach I love it when ya nut up and grab me I feel for ya badly, baby girl just like daddy.

"Shorty I lend my hand out ta help ya, Loss soul looking for shelter, on the late night accept ya," Marlon said as he started to rap the song. "Treat ya good won't disrespect ya. "My age is young, Out of place bitch days is done. From a trixy to a missy you know I raised ya hon. Placed her under my wing, Showed her how we swing. Now she rolling blunts for her king, one day labeled thug Mrs. The essence of my ghetto sisters

Hugs and kisses. That's just for me to be a father figure."

The guys start to laugh and jump up and down as they turn into IHOP's parking lot.

"Bout fuckin time," Carter said as he got out of the car. "I have been craving an omlet all night."

"Quit whining," Tommy said as he opened up the door to restaraunt and let everyone in.

Quez's voice:

By the time we got to IHOP it was 2:15 a.m. and we didn't get to eat until close to 3 in the morning. To the normal person it was just a bunch of kids running the streets and doing kids stuff. To me, it was the defining moment of our friendship. Yeah we didn't get drunk have sex with plenty of woman, partied like a rock star but we went out played video games, talked about our on going life and it took half the night. It was a good thing Omari prevented us from going to the party. Johnny Vargas and his friends were shot and killed by Janine's boyfriend after TA tried to have sex with her. It is really fucked up thinking if any of them were hurt because of pussy. I would not have been able to have these guys be apart of my good and bad times. When we went back to school, all of our lives went a different direction. Tommy went back to UT but in the middle of the semester he decided to travel the world against his families wishes. Before he left, he told me all he has done was school and after school and eventually to work. The day we went to the Alamodome to get the tickets to the Spurs games, he told me he regrets not taking the chance going with us. Tommy said he want to experience the world like we did just wanted to live. After a two year hiatus from school, Tommy changed his degree to IT and graduated Magna Cum Laude. Now he is the head of IT with a major company and has a girlfriend named Jennifer. Even though his family is not happy with his life choices, he says he is happy. Marlon helped lead Tulsa to the Elite 8 but Ronald Curry and North Carolina lit him up. He got drafted by the Nets and got embarrassed by Kobe Bryant in the 02 finals and did not have a good home coming when the Spurs won it all the next year. Despite not having a hall of fame career, he was a two time all-star and was on the Mavericks roster when they beat the Heat in 12. Through his NBA career, Macy was by his side after they made up and was with him since his Jr. year in college. The two have three kids together but never married. Something about they just are happy being together. Omari on the other hand may have a basic life but he is a great example. He graduated from UH and got his Law degree at St. Mary's University and became a good defense attorney. He married Stephanie after graduation plus we were in the grooms party except for Carter, who lost his life to cancer in 2001. The funny thing is he was supposed to die by 1995 but lived six more years. When I talked to him about why he told me not taking the love and support from his family, but the thought of not having an adventure with us would be worth missing. The man was an inspiration because he did not let cancer stop him from doing anything. Because he died so close to graduation, UTSA gave him a posthumous BA in Engineering. We were all there when his mom accepted it in his honor. As for me, well in the season opener of my Jr. year against Mizzu, I went up for a catch on a slant route and the defender took my legs from underneath my me. I fell on my head and suffered a major concussion which ended my possible NFL career. I stuck with the team and was a coaches assistant but got my BA in communications and got my radio show in Maryland. I never married or had children because I was too busy having fun. Thank you Omari and TA for the life lesson. Despite how life has lead us, we are still thick as thieves.

In the present time:

With the summer sun beaming down, no one children are outside because of the unbearable heat. Each of the three friends pull up to a two story home in a nice quiet neighborhood. As Quez got out of his car, he would put his sunglasses on but his face still looks lost. Marlon and Tommy walk up behind him and the three of them walk to the front door. Marlon rung the door bell and a couple of seconds later, a middle aged Stephanie open the door.

"Hey guys, how are you guys doing?" the lady said as she reached out to hug Tommy and Marlon.

"Hey Stephanie, we are doing fine," Tommy said as he let go of the embrace. "How have you been doing?"

"I'm doing fine," Stephanie said as she looked at him and Marlon. Her skin is still has the caramel complection with the inviting smile as she had at 18. When she looked over she saw Quez and cried and embraced him.

"Hi stranger," Stephanie said as she smiled. "When did you get into town?"

"I just got in," Quez said as he let her go. "I went and saw Carter and hope to see Omari. These jokers want to drag me to Mace's."

"He's in the den," Stephanie said as she let the fellas in. The guys walked through the living room and to the family room. The three friends walk up to a glass shelf where an urn with Omari's picture next to it.

"Hey bro, how are you doing?" Marlon asked as cried. Tommy and Stephanie would embrace their friend while Quez stood in silence. Quez collapes as he stared at the urn. Everyone runs to Quez to check on him.

"Quez are you ok," Tommy said as he raises his head and gently slap his face. "Wake up man. Come on get up." Quez opens his eyes and jumps right up.

"Omari you aren't supposed to die!" Quez shouted as he walked to the door to go outside. "This has to be a joke!"

Stephanie runs outside to Quez and grabs his hand as she starts to cry with him.

"Quez, it is ok," Stephanie said. "It is ok. Trust me, but it is ok." The widow gently strokes the freaked out friends arm and looks him in the eyes.

"It is not ok," Quez said as tears continue to fall from his eyes as an April shower. "Why did this happen?"

While he is calmed down by Stephanie, Marlon walks up to Quez and places his hand on his friends shoulder.

"Quez, what is going on?" Marlon said. "Since the funeral, you've been acting weird. Are you going to tell us what happened?"

Quez looks at Stephanie then at Marlon before he made his way to the lawn furniture that is under a shade in the front yard. Tommy sat down on the chair. Quez wipes the tears from his face and lets out a sigh.

"Look, if you all think this is some drama like those stupid ass reality TV shows, you can just forget it," Quez said. "He shouldn't be gone."

Stephanie and Marlon sat down on the lawn furniture.

"Something is obviously bothering you since the funeral," Tommy said. "Talk to me man"

"He pissed me the fuck off!" Quez yelled as he cried.

Sticks and Stones

Two months ago: 3:30 pm EST...

Q*uez's voice*

Just a normal day in the radio world as I was sitting in the studio with my co-host Bart Josephs or Bartty J of the DC Rush Hour show. Barty and I are on different spectrum. I am a muscular black man, while Barty is a chunky white man who knows his things. It is the dream job while working for the radio flagship for the Washington (Commanders) Redskins. It is Cowboys week and I set up a spot where fans from both sides can set up a debate from across the country.

"It was hard loving the Commanders growing up in Texas," Quez said as he is sitting in front of the microphone in the studio. The studio "Everytime they played I would go at it with everyone. From family, friends and strangers on the streets.

"They talk about Troy and Emmitt huh," Bartty J said as he is in front of the other microphone. "That is their go to come back. God I hate these fans. They hop in the delorian and talk about past glories like those guys are going to suit up and play this Sunday." The two radio show host laughs.

"I talk about my friends all the time and one is a die hard Cowboy fan," Quez said. "We didn't start hanging out until 94. Two years later, the Cowboys beat the Steelers in the Superbowl and this joker rubbed it in my face. Well Omari, at least the Commanders have won some playoff games since 1999."

Quez presses a button that plays a "We want Dallas" chant on the radio.

"Yes, yes we want Dallas," Barty said as he laughed. "I hate these fools. It is engrained in my DNA to not like these jokers. My hatred will be passed down to all my kids."

"This is Quez and Barty of the DC Rush hour and this is Cowboys week," Quez said. "We hate the Cowboys and I rather not talk about this sorry ass team but this is a talking point. The final game of the season and unfortunatly the Cowboys are in the playoffs and the Commanders don't know anything moving forward but it is announced they will start rookie Sam Howell. Don't worry cause the Cowboys are gonna Cowboys on Sunday."

"Cowboys are gonna Cowboys?" Barty said as he chuckled. "What do you mean by that."

"They will mess it off as they normally do," Quez said in an aggressive tone. "They always get in the best position and with good teams and find away to f it off. I told this to Omari and he had the gaul to challenge me."

Quez looks up from the computer screen and one of the producers gave him an indication of a phone call. Quez re-adjusts his seat.

"I guess we have fans in the stands wanting to call in but Johnny boy hold the calls," Quez said. "You would not believe some of the things, my friends and I used to do during Redskins and Cowboys week. I mean we all skipped school to get Spurs playoff tickets. Well Tommy didn't go cause he was scared of his parents but Barty do you remember the Sunday Night Comeback."

"The Mark Brunell to Santana Moss connection in the final 3 minutes," Barty said happily as he chuckled. "Who doesn't remember that game? I was smiling when I saw my neighbor cy."

"Well Omari and I made a bet," Quez said. "If the Cowboys won, I would have had to help open up his law office buy wearing a Cowboys jersey and if the Skins won, I would get the green light to date Stephanie's friend Gina."

"The sexy Puerto Rican with the big ass," Barty said as he laughed. "I checked her Instagram page and I was going to see if I can go out with her but my wife would kill me."

"Man I was feeling her since the first time I saw her but thats my boy's wife's best friend and I wasn't going to cross it," Quez said as he sat back up and was in front of the mic. "Gina and her husband got a divorce and she decided to stay up here because of her job. We have been talking every now and then hell we kissed but we told each other not to do anything unless they said it is ok. Let me tell you something Barty, It was me, Omari, Marlon who was about to leave for training camp and Tommy was going through his reach out and touch everyone's hand phase. All game these jokers were getting on me cause the Skins weren't moving the ball and all I kept thinking was not the dirty ass star jersey. Please God no. I think God himself was like, you Cowboy fans need to learn a lesson and all of a sudden bam bam Mark Brunell was on point to Moss. Loved it as much as the 1992 Superbowl."

"Must have shut them up huh," Barty said.

While both are talking into the mic, the prducer is trying to get their attention.

"Oh yes it shut them up and I was going to start up here because I was tired of San Antonio being so damn boring, we all got drunk," Quez said as he looks up and see the producer and waved him off. "When you have friends like that, you want to make sure you keep them. What was even more solid was Gina and I went out before she moved back to San Antonio and Stephanie doesn't know.

"Until now," Barty said as he laughed.

"No she won't know because she doesn't listen to my show, and Omari isn't going to say anything.," Quez said. "I think the secret is safe with us."

"And all our listeners," Barty said. "You know people and social media."

"Eh, but this is Quez and Barty J with the DC Rush Hour and when we come back, we will take your calls," Quez said as he got up from his seat and walked to the producer. "What is it Rion?"

"You have someone who is tieing up our phone lines wanting you to call them ASAP," Rion said.

Quez pulled out his cell phone and saw he had a couple of missed calls and a text message from Omari saying "*Call me now*". Quez called Omari

"Hello," Omari said in an angry tone.

"Whats going on?" Quez said in an annoying tone. "Why couldn't this wait?

"Were you about to tell that story?" Omari said in the same tone.

"No fool," Quez said. "Didn't you hear the whole thing? we got drunk and I loved hanging out with you all. Didn't you hear the fuckin segment?"

"I heard you telling everyone how you wanted to go out with Gina," Omari said.

As Quez walks down the hall he opens a door to go into a stairwell.

"Thats the problem, you are hearing what you want to hear and ready to jump on my case," Quez said. "Do I tell you how to run a trial and get your skanky clients off from going to jail?"

"What the hell does that mean?" Omari shouted. "Where the hell did that come from? Ain't no one trying to tell you how to run your show."

"But you are calling me about what I should say on my show," Quez said. "Like what the hell is your problem?"

"Look I don't have a damn problem!" Omari shouted. "And what the hell do you mean by my skanky clients? I hate to tell you but not everyone is guilty. Unlike you who jump on d's for interviews."

"That trolidyke who falsely accused someone of rape you defended with a bullshit defense is pretty skanky," Quez said. "You are on that Kevin Lomax BS. I got to get back to work"

"Yeah, I got your Kevin Lomax BS," Omari said. "Go back to stroking for interviews." Omari hung up the phone and Quez flung open the hallway door and walked back into the studio to continue the show.

Three weeks later: 10 p.m. EST

A phone rings in the dark, where the only lights come that illuminate the room comes from the street lights and the next door neghbors TV. Quez is startled by the ringing phone and reaches for it on the night stand to see who called.

"Hey Steph, whats going on?" Quez asked. His face turns to shock and drops the phone while he walks to the window where the blinds are partially open. Quez drops to the ground and starts to cry while he falls to the ground.

"Omari!," Quez yells over and over as cries and hits the wall with his fist. "I am so sorry. Omari!"

Present time:

Not one face from the four friends has a dry eye as they sit around on the patio furniture. Quez stands up and walks towards the fence.

"Omari never told me why those two were arguing," Tommy said as he wiped the tears from his eyes. "All he kept saying was everything was going to be alright."

"We see how that worked," Marlon said. "I can see why this is eating him up. I mean why would anyone think Omari would have gotten killed."

"I know what you mean," Tommy said as he grabs Stephanies hand while she is crying. "I didn't want to ask you this but was it true."

Stephanie grabbed Tommy's hand and cried more before she wiped the tears from her eyes.

"This is why I hate the media," Stephanie said as she looked Tommy in the eyes. "If anyone believed his mistress killed him are a bunch of fuckin idiots."

Tommy and Marlon started to chuckle while they wiped tears from their eyes.

"That sounds like something Omari would say," Tommy said. "What happened?"

Stephanie pats his hand and stood up.

"Remember the woman he defended who falsely accused her boyfriend of rape and abuse," Stephanie said as she turned around to look at the guys. Then her face turns to anger. "Ever since he helped her avoid jail time and getting probation, she must have fell in love with him. Omari told me the moment this started to happen and told her probation officer but they didn't do anything to stop it. She would call, email, find him on social media. Hell one time when we were at a concert, she was there. The night he was killed, I heard him shouting and telling her to leave. When I went outside to see what is going on, she pulls out a gun and shoots him three times and two times at me." Stephanie let out a sigh and tears came down her eyes, "He died in my arms while she ran away. I'm glad they caught the dumb bitch."

Quez stomps back to his friends.

"Like I told him, he was on that Kevin Lomax BS," Quez said as he chuckled. "Always trying to save everyone."

"I was trying to understand why you said called him Kevin Lomax," Stephanie said. "Who is that?"

The guys start to laugh.

"Have you ever heard of the movie Devils Advocate?" Marlon asked. "It came out in 1997 starring Al Pacino and Keanu Reeves. Reeves was a good defense attorney even when he knew his clients were guilty he found away to get his clients off."

"When he passed the bar, we started calling him Kevin Lomax cause he said he was not going to help all of his client," Tommy said. "Even if they were guilty. Always saving hoes"

Quez walks over to Stephanie and put his arm around her.

"The last thing we said to each other was so fuckin hurtful," Quez said as he sniffed and cried. "I was to stubborn to call him and say I am sorry I was an assclown."

Stephanie put her arms around Quez to hug him and looks up at him.

"Hey," Stephanie whispered to him. "Look at me."

Since Stephanie is 4ft nothing compared to Quez's 5'10 size, he looked down but had a hard time looking her in the eyes.

"He forgave you the moment you two got off the phone," Stephanie said softly. "He can never be mad at you all. I mean you were the best man at our wedding and been there through all of the times. You all are like brothers to him."

"I know but I can not get past the fact we were so mean to each other," Quez said.

"Bro, do you know how many times I wanted to knock the shit out of you," Marlon said as he walked toward Stephanie and Quez. "I listen to your show and when you bring up some of the things we did, I get so annoyed."

Quez lets go of Stephanie and turns around and walks to Marlon.

"What the hell are you talking about?" Quez asked

Tommy gets up from the lawn chair and walks to his two friends.

"You don't have to tell your listeners about Carter," Marlon said. "Let him rest in peace."

"What?", Quez asked in a stern tone. "What the hell are you talking about?"

"You keep talking about me like I am some damn hippy," Tommy said. "My mom listens to your show and laughs at it all the time."

Quez starts to laugh and grab his shoulders

"Who do you think gave me the material?" Quez said. "Your mom listens to my show and watched all of Marlon's game because she knows two famous guys and a prominent lawyer." Quez let go of Tommy's shoulders and looked at both of his friends. "When I first went on the air and I was talking about you and Rene', she called me that night. She was venting about not getting married and how you were like a hippy. I laughed my ass off because it was funny with her thick filipino accent."

Marlon started to laugh and walk back to the lawn furniture. As the sun started to go down the bright blue sky turn a reddish orange made the summer heat tolerable to be outside. Stephanie walked over to the Tommy and Quez and got in between the two.

"Tommy you don't talk to your parents cause you assume you know how they are but mom is proud of you despite you not being a doctor."

Quez said. "She wants to tell you and hopes Jennifer would be able to go thrifting with her. You know dad is different."

Tommy looked at Quez until he raised his eyebrow at his friend. Tommy nodded his head and the two friends hugged.

"Don't be an asshole," Quez said as he closed his eyes a warm gentle breeze touched his face. "If Omari's death showed me something, it is never take tomorrow for granite." Quez turned around and looked at Marlon. "It isn't promised. I talk about Carter, Omari, and you two all the time because you guys are the best thing in my life outside my parents. You all got me through so much in life so if I talk about it, then yes I will talk about it. Get over it."

As Marlon would get up from the lawn furniture his face he walked back to the friends where Stephanie stayed in the middle of the friends.

"Let Carter rest, man," Marlon said. "His story should not be pimped out for ratings."

"What?" Quez said. "You think I tell everyone about him because of ratings? I talk about all of us because it is to let everyone know how good of a man he was. I tell these stories to keep us alive. Carter's mom loves what she hears. Omari thought I was going to tell everyone that night but I know what to and not to talk about."

Quez closes his eyes as another warm gentle breeze touches his face and he smiles.

"Can someone please tell me what happened that night?" Stephanie asked.

Marlon grabbed her hand and looked her in the eyes.

"Omari got trashed, stripped naked and ran around your apartment complex and," Marlon said as he started to chuckle. "Do you all remember how he was gyrating and calling himself Johnathan Rollins 2.0."

"I'm Johnathan Rollins 2.0," Tommy said as he and Quez gyrated and laughed.

"He was more worried about his reputation being ruined," Marlon said. "He said he was going to take that story to his grave."

While everyone laughed, another soft warm breeze touched everyone as Quez closed his eyes and smiled.

"When I was 10 years old, moms took me to see my grandmother gravesite," Quez said. "I remember mom talking to grandma's headstone like she was right next to her, and she closed her eyes everytime there was a gentle breeze. When we walked back to the car, I asked her about it and she told me everytime the wind blows, a loved one is talking to you." As Marlon, Stephanie and Tommy start to have tears come down their face, Quez grabs Stephanie's hand. "Despite everything I believe Carter and Omari are with us whenever the wind blows."

The four friends hug each other with a strong embrace as a warm gentle breeze touches their backs.

"I love you Omari," Stephanie said as she turns to Quez with tears in her eyes. "Thank you for giving me a different way of knowing my husband is here. I can tell you, he forgave you a long time ago and loved you to death. Thank you for everything." The two grab each others hand as they smile while a gentle breeze wipes the tears from her face. "Oh and I already knew about you and Gina. Why did it take you guys so long to get together?"

"I think I should call my parents," Tommy said as he reaches in his pockets and grabs his phone to call his mother.

Later that night, Quez, Tommy and Marlon are having a good time while they are sitting in the patio of the packed bar and grill named "Carter's" to watch the NBA playoffs. With multiple flat screen TV's on the walls and three in the patio area brings a lot of people to the restaraunt.

"This place is jumping tonight," Tommy said as he faced Marlon. Why is it everytime I come here to eat, they won't charge me?" Marlon turns to face Tommy as he takes a drink of his beer.

"I told them you and the fellas will leave a good tip so just charge him for the drinks," Marlon said. "I own the place and I can back it up. The moment you become stingy with your tips, no more free food." Tommy grabs his bottle of beer and extends it to Marlon as they both give cheers.

"Not a problem," Tommy said as he laughed at him. "I appreciate it." While the three friends sat outside a soft gentle breeze blew in the night air.

"Guess who also comes in when a Spurs game is on TV," Marlon said as he eats a french fry.

"Who?" Quez asked.

"Mrs. Bennett," Marlon said.

As Quez and Tommy have a shock look on their face, Marlon grabs another french fry to eat it.

"Yeah and that is how she busted us," Marlon said.

"What the hell," Quez said. "How did she know?"

"She was at the Alamodome and saw us get off the bus," Marlon said. "She told me when I opened the restaraunt. As usual, she cried when she found out I named this place Carter's and saw a picture we took at the Spurs game." Marlon takes another swig from the beer bottle. "Did you know she is a long time Spurs fan?

"Do she get free food too?" Quez asked as he stares at the TV.

"As long as it is her and not her grubby ass family members," Marlon said. "She got some hard looking kids."

The friends laugh and Quez raises his bottle of beer up.

"To Mrs. Bennett," Quez said. "She is the Alpha of our friendship."

"To Mrs. Bennett," Marlon and Tommy both said as they cling the beer bottles together.

Quez's voice:

As I sit and watch the NBA playoffs, I think about the day we all became close friends and I do not think it was a coincedence but fate. Who would have thought skipping school would lead to a life time friendship. Carter is right. I would miss out on something if I did not have an adventure with these jokers. Even though Carter and Omari are not with us, everytime the wind blows.......